THE TATTOOED INNOCENT
AND THE RAUNCHY GRANDMOTHER

To: Pat
From: Kay &
Wendy

First Edition
(Folio-Autograph, limited to 1000 copies)

Special
Folio-Autograph
Edition

Each copy of this limited edition is
hand-numbered and signed by the author

This is copy

184

Robert F. Cline

The Tattooed Innocent

and the

Raunchy

Grandmother

(An Adult Fairy Tale, Quite Grim)

by Robert F. Cline

Argos House

Acknowledgment is made for lines quoted
from Emily Dickinson's "I taste a liquor
never brewed", Little Brown and Company

"The Boulevard of Broken Dreams" by
Al Dubin and Harry Warren, © 1933
Warner Bros. Inc. Copyright renewed.
Used by permission. All rights reserved.

ISBN 0-9607082-0-0
Copyright © 1983 by Robert F. Cline
Library of Congress Catalog Number 81-69430
Manufactured in the United States of America

First Edition

to
Miya and Teddi
whom I love the most

Inebriate of air am I,
And debauchee of dew.
Emily Dickinson

. . . and Gigolo and Gigolette
Wake up to find their eyes are wet,
With tears that tell of broken dreams.
"The Boulevard of Broken Dreams"

PART I
Introductory

One does not like to think of an innocent as being tattooed.

Neither does one like to think of a grandmother as raunchy.

But herein we shall meet two such.

Ronnie was tattooed.
Millicent was raunchy.

Too, we shall meet some of those whose lives they touched.

Let us hope their story will not offend
your more delicate sensibilities.

11

PART II
Ronnie

1 Innocence

Ronnie, was he really an innocent?

2 Tattoos

Certainly, he *was* tattooed.

3 Tattooed Innocence

He had GRANDMOTHER on a banner in the claws of an eagle across his lower left forearm.

On the buns of his buttocks were TODAY IS THE FIRST DAY and OF THE REST OF YOUR LIFE beneath a brilliant sunrise above his posterior crack.

Over his pubic area blazed I BRAKE FOR ANIMALS, surmounted by a woodland family of bunnies, chipmunks and deer clustered about his navel.

He let all matrons have him — for his heart was large and his soul was kind.

The Author's Reactions

There's nothing wrong with being tattooed. I've often thought of it myself.

But what would my friends think?

Tattooing is artistic.

Sometimes even patriotic.

Yet artistry depends on the artist. Who'd mind being tattooed by Michelangelo? —but Raphael?

It would be my luck to get Ingres: great chunky women pouring water from immense vases swung over their Amazonian shoulders.

Could I face the locker room? —bedmates? —swimming season?

Could I be that strong?

4 Here Comes Grandma
and There She Goes!

Reader, there's enough unhappiness in life without putting more in books.

Thus, preferring the world through rose-colored glasses, I hate to begin with a tragedy of Ronnie's early life.

But it starts with joy, and is too basic to his later development to be ignored, so—

For a few minutes, at the age of five, Ronnie met his grandmother.

It was the only time.

(Since she lived on the other side of town, they never had occasion to meet before or after.)

To Ronnie, this encounter was the highpoint of his childhood—and possibly his life.

It was vision and dream rolled into one, sufficing till his dying day.

Her visit occurred just after dusk.

A glittering whirlwind spun into the house, patted his head, brushed back his hair, tweaked his cheek, asked him if he was a good boy, told him he must always call her Lorrainie Sue—and spun on out the door to dance the night away.

During the spinning, Ronnie had glimpsed a tattooed butterfly gleaming from one shoulder, which was bare.

Never would he forget her high golden hair! —her purple frosted fingernails! —her diamond sparkling dress which floated as it clung . . . and the tiny brilliant butterfly. . . .

A few weeks later, she was killed in an auto accident on the bad curve just outside Ketchum's Corners with her latest boyfriend, Eddie Schwartzenback, returning from the Vegas Palace Dancing Hall.

And, for the rest of his days, Ronnie knew that she watched over him from heaven, sitting at the right hand of God—or, possibly, on his knee.

19

5 Childhood's Happy Days and Happy Ways

Ronnie was born with soft brown hair above soft brown eyes.

The soft brown hair developed a soft brown lock falling wistfully over his forehead. The soft brown eyes developed a soft brown sympathy, often moistening for smaller animals and occasionally for humans.

For instance, they moistened the morning his little pussy Cinnamon Bell was squushed like a slice of deep fried eggplant under the wheels of his approaching school bus, but he drew strength from the times his grandmother had kissed and cuddled him and—pushing the fallen hair from his eyes—climbed the stairs toward the seat alone at the back of the bus to which he'd been assigned because of his head lice.

Across the road was the small square shack he inhabited with his parents. Covered with tar paper for siding, it squatted behind high dust-covered under-brush at the edge of a little-traveled dirt road four miles outside of town.

Within, being an only child, he received the maximum of his mother's attention — intense hatred, revealed mainly through screaming vulgarities and kicks or blows.

Only once had he dared give her one of the notes Mrs. Vlaski sent from school about his head lice.

"I hope they eat your brains out!" she screamed. "If it wasn't for you, I wouldn't be in this goddam mess!"

At such times, his father adjusted the television or headed for the bathroom.

His father ignored Ronnie.

Ronnie yearned for his father.

He could live with vulgarities and kicks and blows, but coping with indifference was hard.

Ronnie slept on a mattress on the floor in one corner of the main room. His parents slept in a bed in a partially partitioned cubicle directly opposite.

At night — during violences of hate or sex, which were hard to differentiate — Ronnie lay pulling at the splinters in the floor and dreamed of the times his grandmother had nestled him within the warmth of her soft and spreading bosoms. (Thus indicating the power of childhood's fantasies, for — actually — Lorrainie Sue's tits had been relatively small and taut.)

Carefully, Ronnie would push the splinters under his

21

fingernails until he could stand it no longer.

Usually, blood came.

Sometimes, when the nights got too bad, he crept out of the house and climbed to the roof.

There, he held out his arms toward heaven and screamed great soundless screams to Lorrainie Sue.

Meals were eaten on the other side of the room at a card table with one bad leg. Usually his parents fought. Sometimes there was only vicious silence. But the television had a roof antenna which could be rotated from inside to receive all channels clearly.

Mornings, carefully quiet, Ronnie breakfasted alone, usually preferring a bread and sugar sandwich with a coke.

Well ahead of time, he crossed to wait for the school bus — stepping through the tin cans, rotting vegetables, torn portions of paper packagings and dog turds of varying consistencies which dominated the debris between the doorway and the road.

Behind him always scampered Cinnamon Bell.

If certain of the dogs were about, Ronnie carried her in his arms.

(Ronnie disliked the dogs who were not friendly playful creatures but skinny, roving scavengers. Occasionally his father petted one, but his mother appeared to hate them almost as much as she hated Ronnie — yet still

22

they hung about the shack.)

In the bus, Ronnie thought of the beautiful funeral service he would hold for Cinnamon Bell when he returned from school. He would tell God what a good kitten she'd been and make a marker for her grave from stones and pieces of wood around the yard.

His brown eyes moistened.

When he reached school, Ronnie headed toward the nurse's office where he was instructed to report each morning because of the chronic infestation of his head.

He hoped he could stay with Mrs. Vlaski all day, instead of being sent upstairs to his classroom where the children called him names like Buggy Boy and Crudsy. (Since his phone had been disconnected for months, Mrs. Vlaski, the nurse, had no way to contact his parents to take him home.)

While Mrs. Vlaski carefully parted his soft brown hair with a toothpick held in each hand, Ronnie told her that his kitten had died. When she said she was sorry, he told her that her name was Cinnamon Bell.

"I named her myself," he said. "She just belonged to me."

When Mrs. Vlaski asked if his mother had given him a treatment before he went to bed, he said: "She had to go out with her girlfriend." When she asked if his father couldn't have done it, he explained, "He wasn't home last night."

23

Mrs. Vlaski sighed.

"Go find your bar of soap," she said. "And don't forget your toothbrush."

Happily, Ronnie headed for her bathroom.

(A few years later, he was to develop a mania for cleanliness which lasted all his life.)

Back home, Ronnie found Cinnamon Bell further mangled by passing cars and covered with buzzing flies.

With two sticks, he pushed her into the ditch beside the road.

Then, kicking a beer bottle ahead of him, he made his way to the front door.

No one was home.

He switched on the TV.

On the kitchen counter, he found a half-eaten can of baked beans.

Eating in front of Mike Douglas helping someone prepare roast duckling with glazed cherry-pineapple sauce, he tried not to think of the flies feasting on Cinny Bell's torn and oozing body.

Instead, he thought of the times his grandmother had taken him to zoos and circuses to ride on elephants and tigers and buy him shiny toys while sipping foamy ice cream sodas.

During the commercial, he got a bottle of coke from the refrigerator.

He hoped his parents would stay out all night.

6 Various Cottages Where
the Rambling Roses Climb

During third grade, Ronnie developed a habit of gulping and gasping when bad things happened in the house.

His mother told him how they felt about his gulping and gasping and refusing to stop.

"I hate you!" she screamed. "And your father hates you even more!" she screamed more loudly. "Don't you hate him, Earl?"

His father, with beer before the TV, nodded Yes.

And Ronnie, still yearning for his father, tried to cease his gaspings.

"Stop!" his mother screamed as he did his best. "Just stop!" Her voice became more shrieking. "Stop! Stop! Stop!"

And doubled in agony, Ronnie tried harder.

Sometimes, especially if alone, he could gain control

by closing his eyes and concentrating on Grandma Lorrainie Sue holding out her arms to him while spinning down from heaven.

Other times, he gulped and gasped till dawn's earliest light came through the little plastic covered window above his bed.

After further violences, his parents told him they were divorcing.

When he mumbled Why, his father headed toward the bathroom.

" — because of all your fucking noises!" screamed his mother.

*

His mother now lived in two rooms at the end of a dark hallway.

At night, visiting, Ronnie would be awakened by quiet snickers or, perhaps, brief screams of louder laughter.

At these times, he liked to open his bedroom door and watch his mother naked with her naked girl or boy friends.

When she saw him, his mother would come and slap him back onto the bed, slamming the door while

26

screaming, "He only lives to torture me!"

*

Ronnie's father also lived at the end of darkness, up five long flights of stairs.

If Ronnie hid under the bed, sometimes his father's groups wouldn't find him.

When they did, his father said, "A good-looking kid like him has to face life sometime."

Why did God make me? Ronnie wondered behind his fallen hair, as they showed him how to play new games.

But later in bed, the answer always came.

"You were made to be loved by Grandma Lorrainie Sue," said the necessary vision in the diamond-sparkling angel's robe which floated as it clung.

*

Foster homes were better.

You didn't have to care about anybody and they usually left you alone when chores were done.

27

Ronnie often had pets, like crickets or a snake in a jar.

At night were happy dreams about the times he used to visit Grandma Lorrainie Sue.

Especially, now, he remembered the warm sweet smells of sleeping with her in her bed.

Between homes, he began to recall how he had lived with her for months on end.

And his only dream was to conduct himself to make her proud — in return for her deep pure love, the rock on which he built his life.

Pretty Bubbles
(Part 1)

Reader, let us hope you sympathize with dreams —
without which life is nothing . . .

. . . for many are the dreams herein . . .

. . . and many are the dreams which make our lives. . . .

write about it!

7 Why Authors Must Speak

Authors must speak because sometimes their characters have difficulty expressing exactly what they want to say. (Authors having no such problem, for are not words their livelihood?)

Take Ronnie, for example.
—so young!
—such a child!
—yet wanting so to speak to you! —so wanting to reach out to you!
Wanting to tell you how blue and clear the sky is. Or could be.
Wanting to tell you to see good things. To hope. To try. To be open, constantly, to change.

And if he were older? And knew you well? And could clearly see within himself?
Then what would Ronnie say?

30

He would say, *Open a gin mill or a neighborhood grocery!*
Get out of that rut!
These are Ronnie's words for you.

Life is *worthwhile,* says Ronnie.

If not, make *life worthwhile!* says Ronnie.

Bankruptcy? you ask.
Go bankrupt! answers Ronnie.
It's worth it.
Hoping and trying are worth it.
They *are* worth it.
They are all that *is* worth it.
Afterwards, go on welfare.
No?
Then try something else! says Ronnie.
But dream that dream, buddy!
Dream that dream! he cries.
And hope! Always hope!
Try! Always try!
Ronnie begs you, *Hope! Try!*

These are Ronnie's words to you.

8 Motivated by a Medium Coke

One day, Ronnie's social studies class was exposed to a screening of *Dr. Strangelove,* leading to profound discussions at McDonald's.

"They say Russian school kids all want jeans," said Kenny Krasselman.

Ronnie listened.

"Underneath, they're probably just like us," said Mike Perotta.

Ronnie nodded.

"Make love, not war," said Will Czankowski.

Ronnie brushed the hair back from his forehead.

"We should invent a love powder and send up satellites to scatter it over the world," said still another.

Ronnie became lost in thoughts as deep as he could ponder.

His brown eyes moistened.

For Ronnie may not have been the brightest boy in the junior class, but he was a feeling person. Very feeling.

And impressionable.

Most impressionable.

Here in McDonald's he was receiving the most indelible impression of his life.

Dimly, near the Ladies' Room, he seemed to glimpse his grandmother . . . smiling as she spun. . . .

9 Ronnie Reacts to Life and the Movies in a Tree

Later, Ronnie climbed high in his favorite tree.

There, he tried to think more clearly.

Vistas were opening toward the heights Grandma Lorrainie Sue would be proud for him to scale.

But the vistas were clouded.

Struggling, he tried to pierce the haze.

Beauty was involved. For did his grandmother not embody beauty?

And love —

Then, suddenly, Ronnie remembered how often his mother had said, "Lorrainie Sue puts out for anything in pants or skirt."

And he knew that what his grandmother put out was love! — all embracing love for all mankind!

(For had he not been enveloped by that same great love from that same great heart?)

34

Thus, dimly, Ronnie glimpsed his fate.

He must spread Grandma Lorrainie Sue's vision of universal love through beauty.

But how?

Aloft midst leaves and soaring branches, he searched for ways to spread his grandmother's vision.

But he could find no path to follow. . . .

10 Birds and Babies Yet Unborn

Ronnie's shoulders, now, were broad.

His hips were narrow.

His eyes probed quietly but could sparkle if unguarded.

On a bronze background, individual features complemented each other handsomely below the soft brown hair in soft brown waves still frequently falling forward.

Girls and certain teachers regarded him with interest.

They found particularly attractive a moistening of his large brown eyes when speaking earnest thoughts.

Also provocative was a new habit, auxiliary to a former.

Brushing his hair back from his forehead, the other hand would drop unobtrusively to check the zipper of his fly.

"I've th-thought considerably about the plight of certain blacks in Africa," Ronnie said to Mrs. Traum in Current History and World Events.

Pausing with emotion, he swept the lock of hair from his forehead.

Then, embarking on hesitant heartfelt comments, his brown eyes moistened as the hand dropped unobtrusively to check the zipper of his fly.

Turned backward in her seat to watch, Monica May Bernstein dreamed of being Gentile to accept his imagined invitation to the prom.

—and, later in bed, Mrs. Traum envisioned the organ which entered her body as being Ronnie's own.

—while, in his bed, Ronnie propped himself over a map on the inside cover of his Modern History text and sighed for blacks in Bujumbura, pesticides on pastures, bums on the Bowery, octopi under oil slicks, and birds and babies yet unborn.

For his heart was large, his soul was kind and his mind sufficient . . . though the love of Grandma Lorrainie Sue inspired him in ways he didn't always understand. . . .

Pretty Bubbles
(continued)

Reader, let us hope you are not only attuned to dreams
—without which life is nothing—but that you nourish
zealously your own . . .

. . . for the only realities of life are born of dreams. . . .

11 Ronnie Encounters
the Divinity Which
Shapes Our Ends

Two weeks later, Ronnie met fate at the New Galena
County Fair.

Beneath the ferris wheel, he stared — transfixed — at
the fading flaps of a dingy side show tent.

Drawn by destiny, he entered.
Within, driven by love and inspired by beauty, he
welcomed pain,
Emerging, LOVE was engraved across the knuckles of
one hand.

Fired with the exhultation of Hannibal entering
upon his alps, Ronnie tossed back his lock of hair in
mighty gesture.
Dry eyed, he sent a joyous gaze on high as if with

power to pierce the veil which separates us from those we love in heaven.

Then he raced home along the shortcut by the railroad tracks.

He had found his fated path!

That night, Grandma Lorrainie Sue looked upon his knuckles with deep pride.

"Would you rather have me spin," she asked, "or clasp you to my bosom?"

"Either would be fine," he answered, in embarassed delight.

*

The following day, the dove of peace was engraved beside his right bicep.

*

Friday, during Pastry-Pig-and-Poultry judging, NOT WAR was added to the knuckles of his other hand.

*

40

Saturday, after the Demolition Derby and before the All Accordion Concert Band And New York Stage Revue, a red rose became clenched in the beak of the dove—its petals opening and closing with the flexing of his bicep.

And later, high in his favorite tree, Ronnie knew Grandma Lorrainie Sue peered down to watch them move.

*

12 Further Steps Along Fate's Path

With the closing of the fair, Ronnie located Ye Salon of Tattoo Artistry in Billings.

Thumb-inspired, he hitchhiked to destiny each Saturday after chores.

Nights, he worked as stock boy in an A&P to subsidize his obsession.

Midst broccoli and endive, Ronnie dreamed of the summits he would scale . . . through tattooed artistry, spreading love and brotherhood to all mankind. . . . .

The Author Feels Constrained to Speak

I must speak!

Ahead, I see problems.

Tattoos cannot be easy to erase.

Suppose a slogan goes out of date? (I think, for example, of "Flower Power" from my youth.)
Suppose an originally exciting concept grows to seem too cute? (There comes to mind a scowling owl, advising "Give a hoot, don't pollute.")
Suppose one feels the simple need for change?— tired of either a part or the whole?
Suppose one alters one's outlook toward life?
—or art?

Bumper stickers can be peeled off.
Or pasted over.
At worst, one finally trades the car.

But tattoos?

I fear for Ronnie.

13 *Kitchen Tables* or
Approaching Manhood, Rapidly

By graduation, Ronnie's body was wholly pictorial and he had risen to delicatessan manager of the A&P, meaning he sliced cheese and spooned out cole slaw.

Older women liked to invite him home for coffee.

He accepted those reminiscent of Grandma Lorrainie Sue.

Sipping the first cup, they would admire his tattoos.
With refills, they would ask him to unbutton his shirt.
By seconds on iced pecan ring or old-fashioned crumb cake, he would accede to their requests that he remove his shirt entirely.
Naturally, then, they had to see the rest.

Which was never a disappointment.

The Author Discusses Sex

Sex is bad.

So very bad.

Beware of horny old ladies.

14 Beneficial Aspects of Fornication or Kitchens Kitchens Everywhere

Yet sex can have its positive side.

All this screwing brought Ronnie's first self-confidence.

Automatically now, at the merest reference to his tattoos, he took off his shirt — to hang it neatly over an adjacent kitchen chair.

He removed his trousers at the slightest provocation.

For exposure brought deep rewards.
Disrobing, Ronnie's stammer disappeared.
Naked, he gained a silver tongue.

And at last he experienced the heady success of seeing his tattoos spread their vision — as Olive Fothergill gave herself to environmental causes, Dottie Delmar embraced the United Way, and the Crayshaw twins — Griselda and Grimalda — turned to the gathering of tuna fish and sweaters for underprivileged children.

15 *Malaise* or *No Bright Skies*

But Ronnie found that a life of sex is a lonely life.

For he had no love.

And Grandma Lorrainie Sue couldn't always heed his calls—being a busy girl herself in heaven.

*

Downtown late one night, Ronnie saw his mother standing in a doorway.

He was going to say Hello, but before he was sure it was her a football player he remembered from high school approached first and Ronnie watched them walk off together, deciding it wouldn't be polite to interrupt.

As they disappeared, he wished he had at least waved.

But she might not have known who he was.

*

47

Another night, Ronnie saw his father pushed out of a bar opposite the bus station.

Yelling curses as he stumbled, he then lay quietly muttering on the sidewalk.

Ronnie's yearning for his father returned, but he decided it was no time to renew acquaintance — which was unfortunate since he never saw his father or mother again.

Perhaps they left town or died.

*

Early in the morning on his next day off, Ronnie walked to the old shack at the edge of the little-traveled dirt road four miles outside of town.

It was abandoned and overgrown.
Peering inside, he did not enter.
Across the road was no evidence of Cinnamon Bell.

He had planned to set up a marker, but the idea now seemed silly.

Nor could he say a prayer.

Walking home, he became sick.

In his rented room, dissatisfaction gnawed.

"Am I truly approaching my dreams?" he asked. "Or

am I just a stud? —available meat for one night stands?"

But what more could he do?

Join a carnival?

(Reader, would you want Ronnie to join a carnival?)

So, like ourselves perhaps, he postponed decision and continued the easier familiar ways.

That afternoon, he visited a few kitchens followed, that evening, by several more. . . .

Further Sexual Comment

Sex is bad.

It can get you all screwed up.

It's too bad Ronnie got involved with it.

A Reader's Viewpoint,
at Variance With the Author's Own

One can get too much of any good thing, except sex.

Additional Comment, from Arkansas

I never get enough.

A Note From Wilkes-Barre

Last night at the drive-in was the best I've ever had.

16 In Which Ronnie Locates
Shirtless Employment Followed
by Emigration to Scarsdale

Ronnie left the A&P—having located a job with a landscaper for shirtless work, outdoors.

For further exposure, he usually labored in cutoffs, wearing them to work beneath his trousers.

But, though passers-by did stop and stare, it was too limited an audience to satisfy his dreams.

Finally, he opted—as youth will—for wider horizons and pastures which might prove more green.

Westchester County is the landscaper's promised land.

Thereto, Ronnie took a Greyhound in the early, early spring. . . .

PART III

The Reader's Role

Discussed by the Author

Enjoy these pages, Reader, yes.

But make it not a passive task.

Readers must work to read, dear Reader!

Clothe the spare bones of my words.

Find, Reader, more than my poor power can present.

Let your imagination soar! —it must exceed the limits of my own!

Reader, in the end, dear friend, be wiser from this book than I!

Parenthetically

(May I hope you feel impelled to read from cover to cover again?

(— to make this even more your own?

(— perhaps to find one small insight into life's insanity, which none of us can comprehend?)

P.S. Have you bought the gin mill?

PART IV
Millicent

1 *Our Raunchy Grandmother*

Millicent is our raunchy grandmother.

2 Was She Always a Raunchy Grandmother?

Millicent was neither always raunchy nor always a grandmother.

3 Then—?

But her life inexorably led to raunchy grandmother-
ness.

Author's Plea

I could have loved Millicent in her later years.

Therefore, Reader, have compassion when first encountering this repulsive child.

4 Behold, a Princess Is Born!

During her earliest years, Millicent was petted and cooed at by two elderly parents who never recovered from the delight of her conception, much less birth.

This occurred in a little white house, green-trimmed, on a shaded street with tall ferns around the porch.

Midst scatter rugs and paintings of forest glades and mountain dells illuminated by vertical shafts of sunlight and small tables holding items made of china, they taught her to feel beautiful and special and so favored by existence that she would always have everything her heart desired.

They took her to supermarkets and restaurants and strolled with her through shopping malls, saying to cashiers and waitresses and window shoppers passing by, "She is our beautiful-little-living-breathing-baby-doll-princess."

Most agreed and cooed at least a little bit.

"I am Princess Millicent," our tiny heroine would proclaim, with curtsy and a dimpled smile.

At a bookstore in their favorite mall, her father found an oversized reproduction of the Duc de Berry's storybook castle.

He hung it at the foot of Millicent's bed.

Millicent would lie for hours imagining herself high in its crenelated towers basking in the adoration of her golden days.

But it was difficult to wait.

5 Poppa's Gonna Buy
You a Mocking Bird

When the tantrums began — in supermarkets, restaurants, and malls — Millicent's mother held her close and shushed and rocked while her father reached in his pocket for the special treats he'd taken to carrying for these occasions.

But cuddling and rocking and Tiny Tootsie Trixies were inadequate substitutes for childhood's golden dreams.

So Millicent continued screaming.

6 *A Violet by a Mossy Stone*

Millicent's bitterness toward the world developed early, i.e., in kindergarten.

Each day her parents brought her to the classroom door—hugging her with reassurances and, usually, a tear.

Always, her hair was primped and her dresses ruffled.

Even the other boys and girls thought of her as a little doll. They petted her and cooed—as did her teacher, Miss Eulalia Ryan, tall and thin and medium in every way.

But sometimes the children had dirty hands, so Millicent pushed them off.

And sometimes Miss Ryan made her sit at her desk writing alphabet letters with a thick black pencil instead of playing with the puzzle blocks, which made her scream from the depths of her tiny breaking heart—for was not she, herself, the center of this new world with its piano and rug and play area in one corner?

Also, being a princess, she liked to order the other children about.

And refused to play outside for fear of dirtying her body or affecting her clothes adversely.

Soon the other children began disliking her.

"Princesses are different," she told herself.

She felt even more special as they turned away.

Princesses grow into queens, she thought, *adored within a marble palace.*

Continuation of an Author's Plea

Try to love my darling, Reader.

Try!

Extend her your humanity, as — if she understood the word — she might extend humanity to you.

For did she make herself a hated, spiteful child? Or was her course — like our own, perhaps — determined by some great omnipotent design?

7 Glad to be Sad

In third and fourth grades, the school psychiatrist was still trying.

By fifth, he had pretty well given up.

Millicent refused to do homework for her teachers because they were *mean*. She hated gym because it was *dumb,* and refused to draw or paint in art. She gave up the viola because music was *boring*.

Having friends is *stupid,* she told herself, walking home alone.

In the house, Millicent and her parents said little.

Mainly, Millicent lay curled on her bed — writing poems about mangled animals and vicious flowers.

In all her life, she could remember no happy moment.

Where were her golden days of adoration in the palace on the wall?

8 *We Gave Her Everything* or
The World Outside the Palace Gates

Finally, inept and confused, her parents sent Millicent to Sweet Briar School For Young Ladies with money they had inherited from Eloise Slump, a distant cousin and last remaining member of the family.

There, Millicent found:

a. silent, morose meals between the ugly duckling of her Introductory Ceramics class and a fat scholarship orphan from Indianapolis;

b. an indistinct and semi-morbid relationship with a divorced physical education instructor, female; and

c. further lonely bitterness.

Still, Millicent had never felt love in any of its varied guises . . . as, with first stirrings of maturity, she yearned impatiently for adoration in her golden days of glory.

*

Before leaving Sweet Briar, Millicent took a maximum of instruction in Personal Grooming and Appearance (Levels I through IV, plus Advanced Independant Study), for artful accentuation of her manifold physical charms.

Her soft alabaster body was entirely warmth and curves, dominated by inviting limpid eyes.

Crowning, her hair swept high — of frequently varying colors.

"Surely now," she thought, reaching for her diploma on the stage, "adoration lies ahead."

And, a vision of beauty, she left for summer resort employment on Cape Cod.

9 Disciple at the
Throne of Love

Millicent now began her marriages.

We will glance only at the first.

He was a business management major who started wild on the beach at Martha's Vineyard — went into his father's business management firm — and ended at ease only with drunks at drunken parties.

(Sex was an especially unimaginative enterprise in his mind.)

"Did you ever really love me?" Harry asked a few weeks before the end.

"Oh, yes," said Millicent. "At first I loved you a lot."

But, divorcing, she told herself it was no more than she'd expected from the start.

71

10 Trivial Affections,
All Trifled

Following a variety of further marriages, Millicent became hostess in the elite Trocadero Room of the exclusive Chez Le Palais restaurant atop a hillside outside Scarsdale.

She was also mistress of a state Supreme Court judge, having previously had affairs with many prominent business men and civic leaders.

All in all, now, Millicent had reached the zenith of regret . . . growing to accept disillusion with a simple ease, and defeat as the truest expectation of existence. . . .

For there were no palaces near Scarsdale.

Further Sorrow for Millicent

Poor Millicent.

One needs something.

So few know how to find it — not even, sometimes, prominent business men and civic leaders.

Auxiliary Author's Note
Of the Self-Revealing Type

Sometimes I'm happy I'm not a prominent business man or civic leader

— but usually I wish I was.

11 Abandoned by a
Supreme Court Judge

Willy, the Supreme Court judge, grew increasingly dismayed by Millicent's genius for unhappiness.

And the ever-changing colors of her hair.

On his wife's death, he decided to take an early retirement option and live quietly in Costa Rica.

"I could never be happy in Costa Rica," said Millicent.

"That's right," said Willy.

So Millicent became ash blond the day he left, also redecorating her apartment in late Wang Dynasty and investing in an emerald green Fiat which she instantly disliked.

But, to her surprise, she began receiving twice-weekly

75

letters from Willy, saying his heart was always with her.

And then he died—leaving her everything, which was an amazing fortune amassed by previous generations of fur tycoons and lumbering giants.

Thus Millicent's life changed drastically.

Before, she had been poor and unhappy.

Now she was rich and unhappy.

What Millicent Might Say

Here, Millicent might jog my arm, saying it's time that she was heard.

Listening, I am surprised how much her thoughts resemble Ronnie's.

For Millicent would remind you, too, "Get out of ruts!"

"Open that gin mill!" Millicent delves within herself to say. "—that neighborhood grocery!"

Then, searching for both insight and the words, "Seek change! Renewal! Growth!"

Thus Millicent would speak—if speak she could from open mind and open heart beneath her newly-flaming bright red hair.

12 A Forgotten Offspring

During one of her marriages, Millicent had had a son.

She had named him J. Humphrey Browne, the *Browne* being the name of that specific husband, the *J* standing for nothing in particular.

J. Humphrey lived with his father, Wentnor Sketherington Browne, who had re-married (as had others of Millicent's former husbands).

Once, years ago, Millicent had been somewhat upset when her son mentioned in a letter that people called him "Humph" instead of "J. Humphrey" or even, simply, "J.H." — an alternative, she thought, both masculine and aristocratic.

Otherwise, it didn't occur to her to think of him.

And of course she didn't bother answering the letter.

So, somewhere, J. Humphrey grew . . .

. . . toward maturity.

13 All Mimsy Were the Borogoves

Being a millionairess, Millicent naturally quit her job to travel through Europe.

But, somewhat to her credit, she grew tired of a life of aimless wandering.

Sitting by herself on the sidewalk terrace of the Cafe de la Paix was lonely.

Reading the difference between Doric, Ionic and Corinthian columns from her Nagel on the Acropolis was dull.

Peering to seek Fujiama through its mists, she shivered with the cold.

Ennui and awe.   Ennui and awe.
                 Ennui and awe.

Was this what life had promised
in supermarkets, restaurants and malls?

Then, suddenly—in Paris and contrary to her nature—Millicent became involved with the possibility of happiness.

It was Thursday at two o'clock in the Luxembourg Gardens.

Millicent came upon children laughing and clapping their hands in front of a Punch and Judy show.

Quickly, she took a plane to Kennedy.

She reclined inundated, in First Class, by happiness.

A grandson would sip hot chocolate on the sidewalk terrace of the Cafe de la Paix with people turning to smile warm glances toward their table.

A grandson would listen enthralled on the Acropolis as she explained Doric, Ionic and Corinthian columns.

A grandson would stand enraptured peering through the mists at Fujiama, then shyly squeeze her hand while gazing up at her with love.

A grandson would bring her adoration in golden days of glory!

14 Remembering a
Forgotten Offspring

Millicent found J. Humphrey in the Manhattan phone book and told him to meet her at Schrafft's.

15 Reunion at Schrafft's

J. Humphrey, dearest," said Millicent, as he and his wife joined her at the table, "I have brought you to Schrafft's for the most momentous decision of our lives."

"Are you really my momma?" said J. Humphrey, tears welling in his shifty little pig's eyes.

"It is time you called me Millicent," said his mother. "Water has passed under the bridge since last we met."

"—thirty-seven years ago in the maternity ward," said Lucette Browne in her usual icy tones of unmitigated hate.

"I have missed you, Momma," said J. Humphrey, bursting into sobs.

He taught high school French.

Lucette stared with hate at her chipped beef with burgundy on patty shell.

84

She was an income tax adviser with H&R Block.

"We are all each other has," continued Millicent.

"Yes, Momma," said J. Humphrey, blowing his nose and pulling himself together like a man.

"I also?" said Lucette, with hatred to her coffee cup.

Then she looked with hatred at the wall.

(Rarely did she look at people.)

"The three of us," said Millicent, reaching out to Lucette's hand which lay dead on the table and covering it with her own.

Oddly, Lucette did not remove her hand.

For whom did Lucette hold her ceaseless and unmitigated hate? For J. Humphrey? (Perhaps, but certainly not wholly.) For Millicent? (Hardly, for they had just met.) For H&R Block? (No, for they were her all in all.) For someone unknown to us? For herself? For all mankind? For the Great Omnipotent Design?

We shall never know.

"You must have a child," said Millicent. "I must be a grandmother."

Lucette's hand turned to stone, but remained beneath the other's.

J. Humphrey stood.

His face grew pale. Great drops of sweat came to his

85

forehead. He began to drool.

Then he turned, stumbling against a chair, and crossed the room—bumping into tables, some occupied, some not—and disappeared out the door.

Lucette reclaimed her hand.

She stood.

Picking up her water glass, she smashed it on a nearby table.

There were several female screams.

Now Lucette's eyes turned to Millicent.

They held damnation's black abyss.

Deep in each glistened a spark of ice.

Millicent feared she might attack.

Lucette withdrew her gaze.

She left.

Millicent sat alone.

No one approached the table.

After a time, Millicent also crossed to the door—paying the cashier as she left.

Walking, she found herself at Bloomingdale's and went inside.

Scenes like this are difficult on Schrafft's.

16 Another Part of Bloomingdale's

Fingering trinkets, Millicent knew she *must* have a grandson.

17 Down and Out in Tarrytown

Reader, must Millicent sink again to bitter depths?

Or, at this moment, do I hear footsteps of her saviour in approach?

PART V

Millicent and Ronnie

1 Templed Hills and
Rocky Rills Ltd

Ronnie was hired by Templed Hills and Rocky Rills Ltd of Ossining, due to the excellence of his recommendation from Buds and Branches of Billings Inc — having well serviced both Bud's wife and Charlotte Branch.

Meanwhile, Millicent had built a palace.

With soaring ramparts and crenelated towers, it was surrounded by a moat with two drawbridges and stood within its own domaine ringed round by far-off craggy summits.

This was just outside Tarrytown.

Millicent derived pleasure from descending its great curved stairways beneath glittering chandeliers, but she longed for the patter of a grandson's feet to bring its marbled soul alive.

Outside, she had installed a free-form swimming pool the size of a Sears Roebuck cafeteria in which she planned to take swimming lessons, feeling it was high time she learned to take care of herself in the water.

During the winter, she contracted with Templed Hills and Rocky Rills for a rocky rill to meander into the pool and a templed hill to accentuate the further shore, along with a wooded glen to rim the eastern coastline.

Work began in late March.

Ronnie was assigned to the templed hill.

Daily, Millicent watched the tattoos on his naked torso. His pectorals and pictorials drove her wild.

Then, with warmer days, he doffed his trousers.

Millicent began supervising the construction more closely.

Ronnie understood.

Her silvery hair and mammoth matronly mammaries were driving him equally amok.

91

2 *Revelation*

Their first intercourse, following coffee with a single refill, was the most supreme revelation either had ever experienced.

3 Hunger

A hunger developed which nothing could assuage.

4 The Surprising Cause

—and it had only been instant Sanka.

Author's Note

Sex. Sex.

I find it deplorable.

Sex. Sex. Always sex.

What happened to stars like Anita Louise and books like *The Whiteoaks of Jalna?*

5 Up Golden Stairs

When Millicent asked Ronnie to become her swim instructor, he said he couldn't swim.

"Good," she answered. "Those who can't, teach."

So, together, midst templed hill and rocky rill and wooded glen, they practiced aquatic skills from an old 1941 Boy Scout Handbook . . . intently supporting each other's bellies while mastering the dead man's float . . . gaily laughing and splashing until they fell exhausted into the waves (installed by Tides and Breakers Inc of Yorktown Heights and Rye).

Reclining on white sea sands trucked in from Montauk Point, Millicent gradually came under the spell of Ronnie's tattoos.

Carefully, she searched his body for hitherto unsuspected details.

"Look!" she cried, one day. "See the smile on the beak of the dove as his rose unfolds with the movement of your bicep!"

"He is happy to give you what he has – both beauty and his love," said Ronnie, pleased that she should notice.

Thus, slowly, Millicent learned to give . . . and so to love. . . .

They often wandered, hand in hand, through flowered glades.

Side by side, they lay on mossy banks.

Watching sunsets, they relaxed high in crenelated towers with wine in pillowed comfort.

Suppers were candle lit, followed by the shared excitements of leisurely baths or showers.

Bedded, Ronnie was overwhelmed by Millicent's softly rolling undulations.

He ran his hand over her snowy bosoms and belly.

"You are a princess," he murmured, devouring those luscious melons with his lips.

Millicent sighed.

"–born for the adoration of a kingdom's multitudes," continued Ronnie, progressing to ultimate regions and lifting his mouth to remove a curly hair.

97

"With you I have found deep, enduring love," said Millicent, sighing still a greater sigh.

"Enduring what?" asked Ronnie, on his knees and gently seeking entry.

"Love," replied Millicent, shifting her buttocks to open her depths to his insertion.

And together, enduringly and deep they probed.

"You bring me my first happiness," gasped Millicent.

"You end my loneliness," was Ronnie's choked reply.

The following week they visited Millicent's lawyer for Ronnie's adoption as her grandson.

Author's Warning

Reader, this relationship may now be entering the area
of legal incest, but keep thinking those happy thoughts!

6 *Preparations for the Fete*

On the delivery of the final adoption papers, Millicent decided to keep the celebration small.

"—just within the family," she said as, spent and sexual member abating, Ronnie withdrew and rolled off her body to lie panting quietly at her side.

Since Ronnie's parents had by now passed into the great beyond (where his mother had been delighted to encounter Lorrainie Sue in an all-night diner patronized mainly by truck drivers), this meant J. Humphrey and Lucette.

7 *The Fete*

As usual, at the sight of his mother, J. Humphrey's little pig's eyes welled with tears and he began to sob.

After introductions and baklava with ponies of Remy Martin, Millicent displayed Ronnie's body.

J. Humphrey sobbed louder at the bunnies, chipmunks and deer.

Seeing the pubic hair intruding into the base of this woodland scene like new-seeded curly grass, Lucette's body flashed with the heat of a flame she had never known.

Her gynecic ductage screamed for Ronnie to fill it.

Millicent announced that she and Ronnie would make the Grand Tour that spring.

8 Sex Visits Lucette

As indicated, sex had just dropped in for his first Hello to Lucette.

9 *Sex Forgets to Leave His Card at J. Humphrey's*

J. Humphrey thought the male appendage was exclusively for peeing.

10 *Lucette Stops By for Sex*

Lucette began dropping in at Tarrytown.

11 Lucette Gets What She Came For

One evening when Millicent was at art appreciation class, Ronnie gave Lucette what she wanted.

After this, she got it bi-weekly, during both appreciations, art and music.

Sometimes she got it during the art of cinematography.

Ronnie could see that Lucette enjoyed these sessions.
Less enthusiastic himself, he hated to deny anyone his body if it could give them a little pleasure — although lately he was beginning to consider excluding males, since they caused certain mental and physical confusions and seemed less appreciative of his tattoos.
And why should he devote his life to sex just to please others?
He had himself to think of.

Slumbering but stirring lay Ronnie's tattoo dreams.

Musings
Recently Discovered Among the Papers of a
Deceased U.S. President and Former Steel Tycoon
Descended from America's First Families
of Wealth and Political Fame*

Buck the system.

Drop out if necessary.

But buck!

Buck! Buck!

Happiness is a good buck!

(Have you had a good buck lately?)

*Endorsed by most prominent
business men and civic leaders.

12 *La Fete Continue*

Between encounters, Lucette gratified herself with
various smooth-handled household implements which
she would warm in water ahead of time and imagine,
with closed eyes, in the form of Ronnie's apparatus, the
whole of which she had memorized by attentive visual
inspection and every tactile means.

While Ronnie and Millicent were in Europe, she further fired her imagination with a series of nude pic-
tures of Ronnie from various angles and in various
states of sexual excitation which he had given her as a
going-away present — having posed for them two years
previously for an iced pecan ring expert who dabbled
in photography.

The Author Apologizes

Believe me, Reader, I don't like this smutty stuff any more than you do.

In rewrite after rewrite, I have cut out dirty, sexy things about these characters — things that almost made me vomit.

But Aristotle urges us to seek the truth. As do the Upshinads and Koran.

In all honesty, therefore, much as I may be repelled by what my pencil writes, I cannot cut further and serve the demands of art.

Why don't you just stop reading?

After all, fiction is only an escape.

Why subvert your moral values for the sake of some cheap, vicarious titillation?

Go buy that neighborhood grocery! Go open up that tavern!

Do something, instead of wasting your time on this.

Above all, keep thinking those good thoughts!

Let them carry you through!

*

Hoping you have left by now, I continue writing for myself alone, for my own ingrown, salacious gratifications.

If you remain, are you any better than the characters of whom I write?

Even Lucette?

13 The Grand Tour

At their sidewalk table in the Cafe de la Paix, Ronnie insisted on Pernod.

"—like Scott Fitzgerald," he said.

And no warm glances were smiled at them from nearby tables—though many did turn to stare at Ronnie's tattoos, while he gazed in awe at this great new world to which he was being introduced.

Later, wandering from the Louvre to Cluny's cloisters, Ronnie felt new longings rise.

These were born of his experience with Lucette.

First, he had been merely pleased that he could get it up with a younger woman.

(Lucette had worked on him for an hour and a half that first art appreciation night.)

Now, along the Boulevard St. Michel, his eyes did not tend to seek out mammoth matronly mammaries.

Instead, they turned toward younger, smaller buds.

*

As Millicent explained Doric, Ionic and Corinthian columns on the Acropolis, Ronnie was distracted by a group of Italian nuns who stopped to point and chatter over his tattoos.

"How can you remember all that?" he asked when Millicent had finished, as a group of swathed Bengalis silently gathered to marvel at his wonders.

That evening, walking the quaint byways of the Plaka, Ronnie waned melancholic.

All he saw was misery and squalor, awaiting Lorrainie Sue's vision of love and brotherhood for all mankind.

Thoughts returned of blacks in Bujumbura, oil slicks plaguing octopi, and birds and babies yet unborn. . . .

Vainly, Millicent tried to capture gaiety.

*

Waiting for the mists to clear from Fuji, Ronnie spent most of his time being privately bathed.

Millicent had him paged as the majestic peak swam into view, but by the time he arrived it had disappeared

111

—so there was no reason for him to squeeze her hand and gaze into her eyes with love.

That evening the Oriental patrons in the crowded restaurant exhibited unbridled enthusiasm over Ronnie's tattoos, many unable to resist coming to the table to examine them more closely.

"Tattoos are a universal language," said Ronnie, standing politely so all could see. "They speak across all barriers."

"That's right," said Millicent. . . .

That night they lay apart in bed, separate and untouching.

Finally, Millicent rose and dressed.

Alone, she wandered the shaded paths of the hotel's dimly-lanterned Oriental garden. Beneath rustling trees, she turned toward the sound of gently splashing waters.

When she reached the waterfall, she could have screamed with anguish.

Instead, she wept in the softly shadowed night.

For no grown man can be a grandson.

In bed, Ronnie prayed for his grandmother.

Lorrainie Sue entered, spinning.

"I love Millicent," said Ronnie.

Lorrainie Sue nodded as she spun.

" — and I do not want to leave — "

Lorrainie Sue shrugged while shimmering.

" — but my eyes have been opened to the world — "

Waltzing in ever-approaching circles, Lorrainie Sue stretched out her arms.

" — and I must spread your vision of love to all mankind."

Cooing, Lorrainie Sue enfolded him to her bosom.

Then she disappeared.

Ronnie never saw her again.

Unfortunately, she forgot to watch over him till his dying day.

*

Thus, still loving,
each lover sensed a future parting

— and the catalyst for that separation was
even then gestating uneasily in Lucette's body —

The Author,
To Any Remaining Readers

Changes are on us.

I sense dark undercurrents . . . modulations to the minor. . . .

But they need not affect you, Reader!

Stock the shelves of your neighborhood grocery!
Polish your bar with lemon-scented linseed oil!
Bring fruition to those hopes!

Reach toward your dreams!

Forge on!

Above all, think happy, positive thoughts!

14 A New Character
Prepares to Enter the Scene

It was during one of her solo trysts with photographs and household implements that Lucette noted the initial swellings of her pregnancy.

First she was surprised.

Then disgusted.

Cupid wounds with his dirty little arrows while the idiot piper pipes gaily on . . . and thus new characters enter our worlds. . . .

PART VI

A Child is Born

1 The Miracle of Birth

J. Humphrey called a taxi to take Lucette to the hospital, since he had senior vocabulary tests to correct.

Lucette was half-crazed as they led her to the reception desk and bordering delirium when they wheeled her to delivery.

But the nurses strapped her to the table extra tightly and eventually she survived the ugly ordeal, successfully purging her body of its indecent burden.

2 *How It Looked and What It Was Called*

The child had soft brown hair which developed a soft brown lock falling wistfully over its forehead, and soft brown eyes which developed a soft brown sympathy—negated, on closer inspection, by a pinpoint of ice deep in the center of each pupil.

Lucette called it Little Lonnie.

J. Humphrey called it nothing.
Sometimes he leaned over its crib with a shit-eating grin, usually drooling on it slightly.
Then he would shrug and go back to correcting papers in front of the TV.

3 Lacks of Suspicion
Regarding Little Lonnie's
True Parentage

No one suspected that Ronnie was Little Lonnie's father.

For one thing, they didn't notice the physical resemblance.

And because *Ronnie* began with one *R* and *Little Lonnie* began with two *L*'s, the names raised no conjecture.

You say Lucette might have wondered?
She *did* think it a coincidence that the two names rhymed.
But it didn't affect her aversion for the child.

You say J. Humphrey might have guessed?
Perhaps.
Or perhaps he thought Little Lonnie was conceived through a sort of osmosis.

120

Because he and Lucette used the same toilet seat, for example.

Certainly, intimacy is implied therein.

And if crabs can be transmitted via toilet seats, why not babies?

Millicent was too excited to think about anything.

Ecstatically, she outfitted a nursery to accommodate the baby's visits.

Ronnie was too busy suppressing and acknowledging his tattoo dreams to realize the child existed.

And of course he'd never seen it. . . .

4 Caring for a
Newborn's Future

Little Lonnie was six weeks old on Mother's Day.

By then, J. Humphrey and Lucette were happy to give him to Millicent.

Fittingly, the transfer of ownership took place at Schrafft's.

"It was the nicest present we could think of," blubbered J. Humphrey, cold drops of water running from his armpits down his sides in delicious fear that Millicent might kiss him. "Besides," he added, drooling heavily, "what would we do with it if we kept it?"

Then he began to fall apart.

Staring with hate at a nearby chair, Lucette passed Little Lonnie across the table.

Millicent took him.

"All my own!" she cried. "And little, like a grandson should be!"

Joyously, Millicent left.

Cooing at Little Lonnie in her arms, she headed home without a thought for Bloomingdale's.

This incident had been much easier on Schrafft's.

5 Greetings and Farewells Between Lovers and Grandmothers and Fathers and Grandchildren and Sons (and, Possibly, Brothers)

Fearing the end yet eager for new beginnings, Ronnie opened the door.

Millicent entered, carrying the baby.

It gurgled happily.

Millicent could not disguise her joy.

"Look," she said. "He might be your brother. His hair is soft and brown like yours and he even has a lock."

And, looking, Ronnie saw this was his son!

The baby made more happy noises, holding out its arms.

Ronnie headed for the bathroom.

Slowly, Millicent carried the baby to the nursery.

Returning, Ronnie watched TV.

*

At suppertime, Ronnie—previously packed—was gone.

On the table was a note.

Millicent picked it up.

It said, "Our love is forever."

Millicent stood staring at it.

Then, putting it in her pocket, she went to ask cook to serve her supper in the nursery.

The Author Speaks, Sadly

Ronnie and Millicent
having gained true love
must part.

For 'tis said that life has greater heights to scale than
those of love. . . .

PART VII

Ascents to the Heights

or

Separate fulfillments of their dreams for Ronnie without Millicent and Millicent without Ronnie, yet written together contrapuntally somewhat in the manner of Bach or Vivaldi, both of whom the author could do without, preferring Berlioz or Mozart or Verdi and some Schubert, especially that inspired and never-elderly warhorse, his 8th —but no Beethoven, please, his inspiration and wit never having approached the Beatles'

1, 2, 3, 4 and 5 (contrapuntally, as promised) *Facing Freedom, First Steps on New Paths, Scaling Heights, Attaining Summits, and Self-Fulfillment—with Queries by the Author and, He Hopes, the Reader*

Forgetting his son, Ronnie was fired with enthusiasm to achieve his tattoo dreams . . . in addition to exploring his new-found interest in younger women.

*

Millicent, too, faced the future in fervored anticipation.

With the grandson of her dreams.

And her genes.

(She thought.)

128

And little, like a grandson should be.

*

Ronnie saw he must start again from scratch.
Clearly, many of his tattoos were faded.
Some were out-dated.
Others were not of the perfection to which he now
aspired.

*

Oddly enough, Millicent did excellently with diaper
changings, bottle warmings, and screamings in the
nights' wee hours.

*

Ronnie entered a private cosmetic surgery hospital
patronized mainly by actors and politicians.

*

Millicent studied books on child psychology and enrolled in workshop seminars for new mothers.

*

Ronnie emerged from the hospital with a totally unblemished corpus, burnished to a deep clear gloss.

*

Happily for Millicent, Little Lonnie proved a pliant child.

Carefully, she molded this clay descended from her own loins via J. Humphrey.

(She thought.)

*

Now Ronnie traveled to the most noted artisans in the world including Yokahama, Buenos Aires, San Diego, Amsterdam and Stalingrad.

*

Millicent submerged Little Lonnie in the flooding ocean of her love.

Endlessly, she cuddled and fondled.

Ceaselessly, she petted and pampered.

In return, Little Lonnie kissed and clung.

*

Ronnie had the youngest and most beautiful women in the world.

(They grew, especially, younger every day.)

*

"Grandma loves Little Lonnie," whispered Millicent.

"Little Lonnie loves Grandma," replied the boy.

"Soon the Grand Tour," continued Millicent, as they lay in bed caressing.

*

131

Finally, Ronnie was a joy to behold.

The embodiment of beauty, he was art's supreme achievement.

For example, the acclaimed LOVE AND BROTHER-HOOD bas-relief between his shoulders was acknowledged to outshine all previous efforts by Praxiteles, Picasso, and Frank Lloyd Wright combined — though, on actual inspection, it was but a single richness within a total field of unimaginable richesse.

It was often said he was impossible to digest on a single visit.

*

While Little Lonnie sipped hot chocolate on the sidewalk terrace of the Cafe de la Paix, Millicent acknowledged with slight inclinations of her head the warm glances smiled from every side.

"This is the best hot chocolate in the world," said the boy, coming to cling about her neck.

And Millicent's heart soared upward.

*

Subsidized by midwest art leagues, Ronnie swept the prairie states.

Next he stormed the east coast and the west.

Now continental art museums rallied for triumphal European tours, while Asiatics clamored for his presence.

Exalting, Ronnie stood naked and silver-tongued before Patagonia's cheering throngs.

*

On the Acropolis, Little Lonnie listened enthralled as Millicent discussed Doric, Ionic, and Corinthian columns.

"Promise to tell me more tomorrow," he begged, snuggling to her bosoms.

And Millicent rose to further heights.

*

Finally international conclaves rose, to spread Ronnie to each nook and cranny of the world.

His tattoos spoke to the multitudes.

133

And the multitudes reacted.

*

Millicent's hand in his, Little Lonnie gasped with rapture as Fuji swam to view behind its swirling mists.

Then, squeezing her fingers, he gazed up at Millicent with love and said, "You are the best grandmother in the universe."

And, burying his head between her thighs, their bodies blended — Little Lonnie experiencing his first erection and Millicent approaching the zenith of all ecstasy.

*

Joyously, Ronnie called mankind toward brotherhood and love — from pigmy chiefs to plumbers, from Irkutsk to downtown Santa Fe.

Yachting off Madagascar, an oil tycoon considered promoting solar energy.

In Michigan, two congressmen nearly voted for the best interests of their constituents.

A black, named Brown, arose from misery in Bujumbura and in remotest haunts of southwesterly octopi, the waters grew a bit more clear. Though bums danced not yet in happy plenty through the Bowery, pesticides on north Tibetan pastures thinned.

Soon earth would be a better place for birds and babies yet unborn. . . .

*

WRITE ABOUT IT !

Pretty Bubbles
(Part 3)

Rejoice, Reader, for Millicent and Ronnie!

For they have touched their dreams!

Which few do. . . .

P.S. And you?
　　　　The little tavern?
　　　　That neighborhood grocery?
　　　　— and you?

PART VIII

A Quick Glance at J. H. and Lucious Lucy

1 *J. Humphrey Forges Onward*

J. Humphrey continued firing the imaginations of high school juniors with subjunctive forms of irregular French verbs.

2 *Lucette Faces Life*

Lucette urged her clients to keep detailed daily tax records, warning of direst consequences for failure to do so.

3 J. Humphrey and Lucette Ensemble

Together, J. Humphrey and Lucette thought rarely of each other and never of Little Lonnie.

Sometimes, J. Humphrey thought of Millicent. At these times his little pig's eyes would well with tears and, in the high school cafeteria or in waiting lines for movies, he would burst out sobbing.

Sometimes Lucette thought of Ronnie. At these times, she headed for various household implements.

PART IX

Descents from Glory

Still Separated, Ronnie and Millicent Fall from the Heights They Have Attained

(Again told polyphonically, but without reference to Brahms or Tchaikowsky, neither of whom the author has ever really given a chance—not, however, feeling the less for it.)

1, 2, 5 and 6 (A depressing
melange, all untitled; with 3
and 4 deleted as too dirty.)

Like Glen Campbell or Ramon Navarro, Ronnie's
star began to wane.

*

When Little Lonnie reached fourteen, Millicent's
problems began.

*

Yes, Ronnie found the world grows tired of those it
loves—seeking novelty, not beauty . . . unable to
assimilate thoughts of universal love. . . .

142

*

By fifteen, Millicent could barely cope.

*

Forgetting Ronnie, earth resumed its normal paths.

*

Millicent watching, Little Lonnie matured oddly.

*

Ronnie saw blacks return to misery in Bujumbura while oil slicks thickened over even the most southwesterly haunts of octopi.

*

Gradually withdrawing, often Little Lonnie would not suffer Millicent to touch him.

*

Ronnie abandoned his hopes for Bowery bums and pesticides on pastures.

He dreamed no longer of a better world for birds and babies yet unborn. . . .

*

Millicent lay reading books in bed or paced the halls or sat uneasily in chairs, as Little Lonnie disappeared into secret passageways within the palace walls.

For days, sometimes, he only appeared for feedings.

At these times, he did not speak.

In his eyes, Millicent saw specks of ice, grown wild and strong.

*

Ronnie's burnished gloss began to dull.

*

Millicent followed muffled shrieks within the walls, culminating in moans which echoed from all directions. Then came long silences as Little Lonnie violated himself with vicious savagery.

*

Ronnie grew tired of the world.

*

Helplessly, Millicent saw Little Lonnie start to roam — as, slowly, his inner viciousness turned outward.

At a nearby farm, a mother duck and her five fluffy ducklings were found with their heads twisted off their bodies — Little Lonnie having been seen, earlier, standing at the edge of the pond.

145

*

Ronnie developed a paunch and pouches.

Young women no longer wanted to enter his bed.

*

Next, Little Lonnie turned himself toward people, usually small.
Millicent made large payments to ward off suspicions, especially in cases of loss of bodily functions or death.

*

Certain of Ronnie's marvels sagged.
Some grew blurred.
Others cracked.

*

Millicent lost weight.

Her color drained.

Deep lines came to her face.

She resorted to excessive makeup, which made her look grotesque — many assuming her mind was odd.

*

Ronnie's thoughts became confused and dark.

*

After the incident of the razor blades — following, as it did, so closely on the incident with the acid — the judge ordered Millicent to have Little Lonnie attended to.

Millicent sent him to an institute outside Detroit.

*

Ronnie began to dwell on the past . . . and on the son he'd lost. . . .

147

(A DEPRESSING MELANGE, UNTITLED)

*

Millicent poured herself another Remy Martin. . . .

*

Ronnie wandered . . . unrecognized, unshaven and unkempt. . . .

*

PART X

The Lower Depths

1 Return to Innocence

On the grounds of a newly-constructed community college where formerly ran a little-traveled dirt road about four miles outside of town, authorities discovered Ronnie constructing a neat pile of stones and sticks while mumbling prayers.

They telephoned, collect, to Millicent whose address was in his wallet.

2 Forever Wilt Thou Love and She Be Fair

Barely recognizing him, Millicent led Ronnie aboard Northwest flight 234 for Tarrytown.

Glancing sideways she was repelled by the translucent yellow of his face, with deep-sunk eyes in blackened hollows.

Finally realizing who she was through caked rouge and thick mascara, Ronnie mumbled "I want my son."

Millicent strapped his safety belt as they taxied up the runway.

"I want my son," said Ronnie. "You took him from me."

Millicent leaned back, looking out the window.

By the time the great shores of Lake Erie appeared below, she understood the truth:

Ronnie was Little Lonnie's father!

The grandson in whom she'd invested her life was not her grandson at all!

Signaling the hostess, Millicent ordered a Remy Martin but had to settle for Martell's.

Ronnie slept, occasionally making small whimpering noises in his dreams.

3 Togetherness

At the palace, Ronnie did not react to suggestions that he wash or shave or change his clothes.

"All I want is my son," he said.

Millicent explained again.

"He had problems," she said. "I sent him to an institute outside Detroit."

"I want him," said Ronnie. "He's my son. We'll live together on a South Seas isle."

4 Love Conquers All

Ronnie wandered through the castle, collecting splinters of wood which he stashed in the upper pocket of his shirt.

Watching TV, Millicent shuddered as he forced the splinters under his fingernails until they oozed blood.

Ronnie started stammering as he spoke.

He began to gulp and gasp.

He took to fingering his fly.

One afternoon, he removed his clothes and roamed the castle exhibiting his ravaged tattoos to the servants, whom he urged to follow him toward love and brotherhood for all mankind.

It was an ugly sight.

Late one night, cook spied Ronnie on the roof of the highest crenelated tower—holding out his arms toward the sky and calling to someone to help him find his son.

Terrified, she woke the gardener.

With his eldest son, he brought Ronnie safely to the ground.

Throughout this period, Ronnie became most coherent when speaking of Little Lonnie.

"You took him," he said, approaching Millicent's lounge chair on the terrace. "Now I want him back."

With some fear, Millicent again explained about the institute.

"I want him," said Ronnie. "He's my son. We'll find happiness playing frisbee on a tropical isle."

"He went bad," sobbed Millicent, finally breaking down.

Millicent was at her wit's end.

Thoughts of April in Paris were all that kept her going.

She had made her hotel reservations the previous fall.

*

Carefully screening applicants, Millicent hired two muscular attendants to watch over Ronnie, stressing that they keep the drawbridges raised at all times

155

except for regularly scheduled deliveries, when they were to confine Ronnie to his room no matter what the circumstances.

Then, well-nigh frantic for chestnuts in blossom, she boarded a Concorde.

Arriving, she found the heart of Paris somewhat warm and gay

— though less so than she'd hoped.

5 Shades of Gertrude Ederle

Millicent hadn't realized how accomplished a swimmer Ronnie was, having improved on the basics of the 1941 Boy Scout Handbook in YMCA's across the world during travels at the height of his fame.

Before daybreak, while the muscular attendants were in bed making love, Ronnie swam the moat — floating his clothes ahead of him in a plastic boat in the form of a whale — and received a ride in a pickup truck to Ossining where he was barbered, shaved and newly-outfitted on Mastercharge.

On the plane, his brown eyes moistened at the happiness ahead. . . .

6 United at Last!

In the visiting parlor of the Midwestern Rehabilitation Institute for Young Men and Boys, Little Lonnie sat on the edge of the room's only sofa, occasionally chewing at his fingers.

Ronnie pulled up a straight-backed chair.

Leaning toward the boy, he said, "I am your father."

Little Lonnie glanced up.

"We can go away —" said Ronnie.

Little Lonnie stared at him.

" — to find happiness —"

Little Lonnie leaned forward.

" — on a South Pacific isle."

Little Lonnie reached in his pocket, pulled out a switchblade knife, and sprang at Ronnie.

Guards, hearing, managed to subdue the boy.

"We offer no hope," said Dr. Tressner, in his office.

Ronnie headed for the airport in his rental car, dimly aware of further steps that he must take. . . .

7 Compelled to Board a 747

Changing planes at Kennedy, Ronnie now stared clearly through the cabin walls to necessary action.

Again, his brown eyes filled with moist anticipation. . . .

8 Ronnie Takes Care of Millicent's Problems

Preparing for an afternoon nap in the depths of loneliness in her hotel room in Paris, Millicent was overjoyed at Ronnie's arrival—especially since he'd cleaned and shaved.

Ushering him into the room, she experienced a tingling of the old Sanka feeling.

Re-draping her negligee over one shoulder, she stepped back to view him more clearly.

He almost seemed to smile.

Millicent felt a wild surge of hope.

Ronnie set the gasoline can on the floor, blinked the moisture from his eyes, and brushed the lock of hair back from his forehead.

Then he bound and gagged Millicent.

161

Next he saturated her with the gasoline and lit it.

Her last words sounded like "Lonnie"
   — or maybe "Ronnie"
   — repeated twice
   — but muffled because of the gag.

(Thus, Reader, I can't be sure.)

The stench of Millicent's burning attracted a passing chambermaid, so the hotel was saved.

Goodbye to Millicent

Adieu, dearest princess!

You waited long for golden days — and passed through them so swiftly. . . .

Godspeed, my little dimpled darling.

'Twas not your fault.

And all of us here at the party want you to know we understand.

9 Compelled to Further Action

Ronnie caught the next flight to New York.

10 Ronnie Attends to
J. Humphrey and Lucette

Hallelujah!" screamed Lucette as Ronnie entered, hurling herself against his groin and clawing. Then she collapsed at his feet, writhing and panting on the floor.

Reaching across her, J. Humphrey took Ronnie's hand in his hot moist ones, blubbering that they hadn't seen Millicent since giving her the baby in Schrafft's.

Then, turning away, tears welled in his little pig's eyes and he burst into sobs as—drooling heavily and stumbling over Lucette—he fell apart before he could reach his chair in front of the TV.

Ronnie set down his tool case, brushed the lock of hair from his forehead, and blinked the moisture from the blackened hollows of his eyes.

"I've come to take care of you," he said.

165

He did this in a little-known Oriental manner, involving their private parts.

Poor dears.

It wasn't very nice.

*

At least they were together at the end.

*

Farewells to a Lovely Couple

Goodbye, J. Humphrey—you'll drool no more bewildered. . . . So long, Lucette—may you find good sex in heaven.

11 Final Compulsion

Ronnie had another plane to take.

12 Reconciliation

The Institute being staffed by a skeleton crew in the nights' wee hours, Ronnie readily gained admission by a reference to Dr. Tressner and a large bribe to the head guard at the gate.

Entering the room, he found Little Lonnie in peaceful sleep.

Ronnie rolled his overcoat into a ball and held it pressed to his son's face until the thrashing stopped.

Now he lifted Little Lonnie in his arms, cradling the smaller body to his own and covering its face with kisses.

Then he lay the boy on the bed and, kneeling, brushed back his lock of hair and gently closed his staring eyes.

Now Ronnie remained quietly for some time, gazing

into his son's face and occasionally stroking his cheek with his fingers.

*

Nodding to the guard, Ronnie passed through the gate.

Driving to the airport, he began to gulp and gasp so hard he had to pull up on the shoulder of the road.

Auf Wiedersehen to Little Lonnie

Goodnight lad, destroyed so early. . . . Was there the possibility you could have become the best of all?

13 *Transition* or
A Poor Choice of Seats

When he finally reached the airport, Ronnie's gulping and gasping had almost stopped.

Airborne, he stared vacantly ahead, responding to no questions by the hostess.

Eventually, the lady next to him moved to another seat.

But, by the time the pilot announced they were crossing the Mississippi, Ronnie felt much better.

And soon after leaving St. Louis, he was able to order his meal without a problem.

PART XI

Terminal

or

Ronnie Gets Off the Bus Alone

1 On the Bus

Traversing Kansas, Ronnie read about the deaths in an Evening Gazette he found stuffed between the seats.

First he was shocked at the manner of the killings.

Next, he felt a sadness for these people he had known.

But the newspaper was two days old, so he didn't feel that badly.

He did, however, shake his head at certain memories.

There were good times, he thought, *and there were bad.*

Then he looked out the window at yellowing fields and a few green trees.

2 *And Miles to Go Before I Sleep*

Ronnie spent the rest of his life in and out of small town jails for molesting little girls.

3 End of the Line

Ronnie was alone at death, vomiting into a jailhouse john.

4 *Speculation*

Did he briefly think of Millicent? or Lorrainie Sue? or tattoo fame? or Cinny Bell?

Does it matter?

Bewilderment

Does it matter?

A Plea

It *must* matter!

Requiem Aeternam

Farewell, Ronnie, and peace unto your soul.

You were our hero, and tried as you could, sweet prince.

You were as good as life allowed.

You knew love, Ronnie, and touched your dreams.

You had good times, and bad.
Can one ask more?

May you meet your grandmother in heaven.

I, for one, shall miss you here.

Farewell.

*

The Author, Again, To All Remaining Readers

Hi!

How's the neighborhood grocery going? or that little tavern?

Have you thought of doubling the value of manufacturers' coupons on Wednesdays? or featuring a reduced price Happy Hour from 4:00 to 6:00?

Keep plugging, baby!

Keep bucking, boy!

Above all, keep thinking those happy thoughts! — those real good happy thoughts!

A Comment

Too bad things had to end so unpleasantly for everyone.

Pretty Bubbles
(concluded)

Reader, this has been a book of dreams—without which life is nothing—

Some dreams were touched—some never touched—some touched, then lost.

But are dreams meant to be clasped and held?

Old dreams fade and new dreams rise . . . until all bubbles burst with final rest, releasing us from our anguished search for dreams forever. . . .

A Personal Question,
Somewhat Embarassing to the Author

Are you going to read it again?

I can't help asking.

For I still feel you to be wiser than I.

And surely there is an answer to life's insanities.

When you find it, drop me a line.

Well . . .

It was nice meeting you.

I like you so much I hate to leave.

And don't worry about those people.
I just made them up, anyway — except for their filth.

I'm really sorry about all their filth.

Finale
'Till It Be Morrow

So long!

*

Happy days!

*

Keep in touch!

*

Goodbye. . . .

*

Epilog

Life's a bowl of cherries!

Oh yes . . .

Oh yes . . .

Oh yes. . . .

ABOUT THE AUTHOR

Robert F. Cline has always lived on a small lake outside the resort town of Saratoga Springs in the foothills of the Adirondacks.

He studied at Williams, Columbia, Yale, Tufts, and the Paris School of Music.

His background runs the gamut: stage manager in New York's off-Broadway theatre, comic book writer, director of contract bridge tournaments, folk singer, wine steward, teacher of music and French and classical guitar, cryptographer, gambling house doorman, construction worker, waiter, army sergeant, publicity man, occasional actor, salesman of overpriced designer neckties, and grapefruit trimmer.

Born Robert Cline Miyamoto in 1924, he is the father of two daughters, his life's joys.

A confirmed traveler, his favorite places are Paris and London, the Aegean islands, Venice "or anywhere in Italy", Haiti, and New Guinea.

He likes skiing, Verdi, Scott Fitzgerald, camping, Berlioz, Fielding, gothic cathedrals, Frank Loesser, old movies, Bessie Smith, *Alice in Wonderland*, spaghetti, Wordsworth, World War I songs, and friends.

Possessing a happy and positive outlook on life, Robert Cline hopes you will not confuse him with the somewhat odd imaginary author who narrates his book.